This book belongs to

Beth Wunderlich 2010

©2006 Big Idea, Inc.

"None of you should look out just for your own good.
You should also look out for the good of others."
Philippians 2:4

Published by Scholastic Inc., 90 Old Sherman Turnpike, Danbury, Connecticut 06816.

ISBN: 0-7172-9841-8

Printed in the U.S.A.

First Scholastic printing, February 2006

A Knight to Remember

A Lesson in Kindness

written by
**Cindy Kenney
& Doug Peterson**

Illustrated by
**Greg Hardin
& Robert Vann**

SCHOLASTIC INC.

New York Toronto London Auckland Sydney
Mexico City New Delhi Hong Kong Buenos Aires

It was a night to remember in the Kingdom of Scone. Hundreds of Veggies strolled into the castle's courtyard to watch the annual Tournament of Pies. Excitement was in the air, and so was the sound of music.

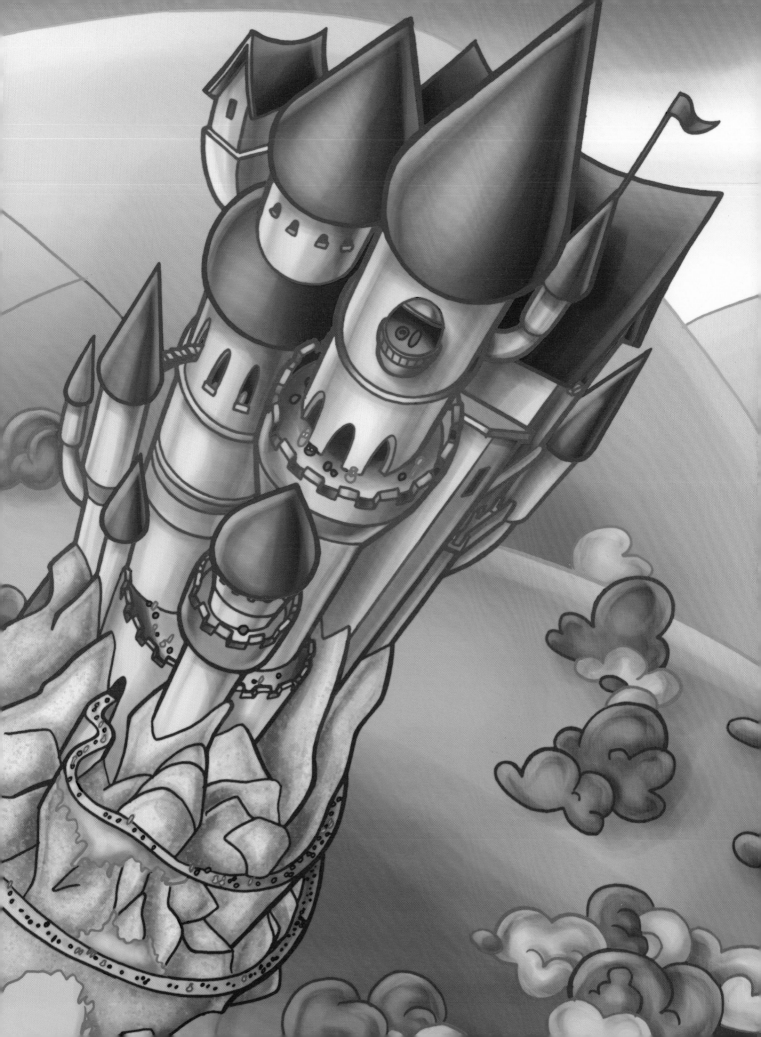

"Bye, bye, Miss Rhubarbarian Pie. Drive your vassal to the castle and—"

Bonk! A singing pea swung his mandolin to and fro and chuckled.

"Ouch!" Petunia cried, as she quickly dodged another smack from the mandolin.

Several Veggies turned to see what happened, but Petunia quickly lost herself in the crowd. The Kingdom of Scone didn't like people from the Kingdom of Rhubarb.

She hurried into the Tournament of Pies stadium and sat in the Fair Maiden section. Various knights were getting ready for pie contests that required bravery, skill, and a variety of tasty, mouth-watering, delicious pies.

The band played a little knight music as the master of ceremonies announced the first contest. "The first pie competition this evening is between the Silent Knight and the Knighty-Knight!"

The crowd became quiet as the two knights hopped up to a table loaded with pies. When the queen stood and gave the signal, the pies flew. Coconut Cream! Chocolate! Even peanut butter!

Pies splattered against each knight's shield. But neither knight was creamed until . . . **Splat!**

A pumpkin pie sent the Knighty-Knight home to bed.

The crowd roared their approval and the Silent Knight was silent no longer.

"I am the greatest!" he boasted to the guy from the Knightly News. "I will finish **FIRST** before the day is over!"

But while everyone cheered the winner, Petunia watched something else. Another knight slipped into the stadium and helped the loser back up.

"Who is that?" Petunia asked a nearby carrot.

"That's the Duke of Scone!" the carrot laughed. "Don't you know anything?"

As Petunia shook her head no, another carrot turned to say, "She wouldn't know that, because she's a **Rhubarbarian.**"

Then the carrots turned their backs on her.

The announcer once again stepped up to the microphone. "The second pie contest of the day features that knight who always has a fever…the Saturday Knight!"

The crowd clapped and cheered.

"The Saturday Knight will face a knight who's known for always running behind…the Late Knight!" As applause filled the stadium, everyone paused to look for him. But he was late, of course.

When the Late Knight ran in the door, the Queen stood to begin the contest. Pies were splattered in an ooey, gooey, sticky, icky **mess!**

"I'm stayin' alive!" the Saturday Knight proclaimed.

"Not on my watch!" called the Late Knight.

When the crust settled, the Saturday Knight was creamed clear to Sunday. He lay flat on his back with custard plastered on his face.

The Late Knight teased the loser, who crawled off the field in shame. "You're nothing but a knight-crawler. But **I AM THE GREATEST.** When this day is over, I will be **FIRST!"**

As the crowd cheered
the knight's victory, Petunia
once again kept her eyes on the
loser. The Duke of Scone hopped into the
stadium to help him up and wipe the pie from his face.

More contests followed as knights catapulted pies, shot them with crossbows, and
even battled in a free-for-all. And after every contest, Petunia noticed the Duke of Scone
was always there to help the loser.

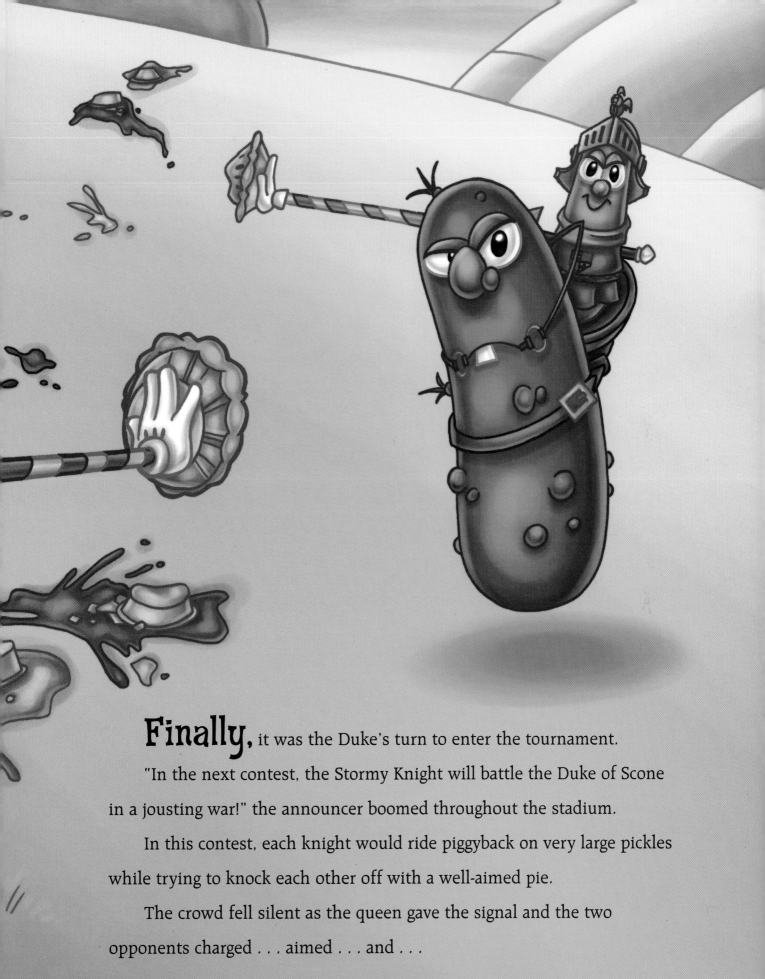

Finally, it was the Duke's turn to enter the tournament.

"In the next contest, the Stormy Knight will battle the Duke of Scone
in a jousting war!" the announcer boomed throughout the stadium.

In this contest, each knight would ride piggyback on very large pickles
while trying to knock each other off with a well-aimed pie.

The crowd fell silent as the queen gave the signal and the two
opponents charged . . . aimed . . . and . . .

Missed!

The knights once again lined up to face each other. The queen gave the signal and each opponent charged again. As the knights raced toward each other, suddenly...

"MOMMY!"

The sound of a little carrot could be heard from the crowd. The Duke tried to ignore it, but as he prepared his pie . . .

"Mommy!"

The Duke turned to see if he could spot the child. And as he did . . .

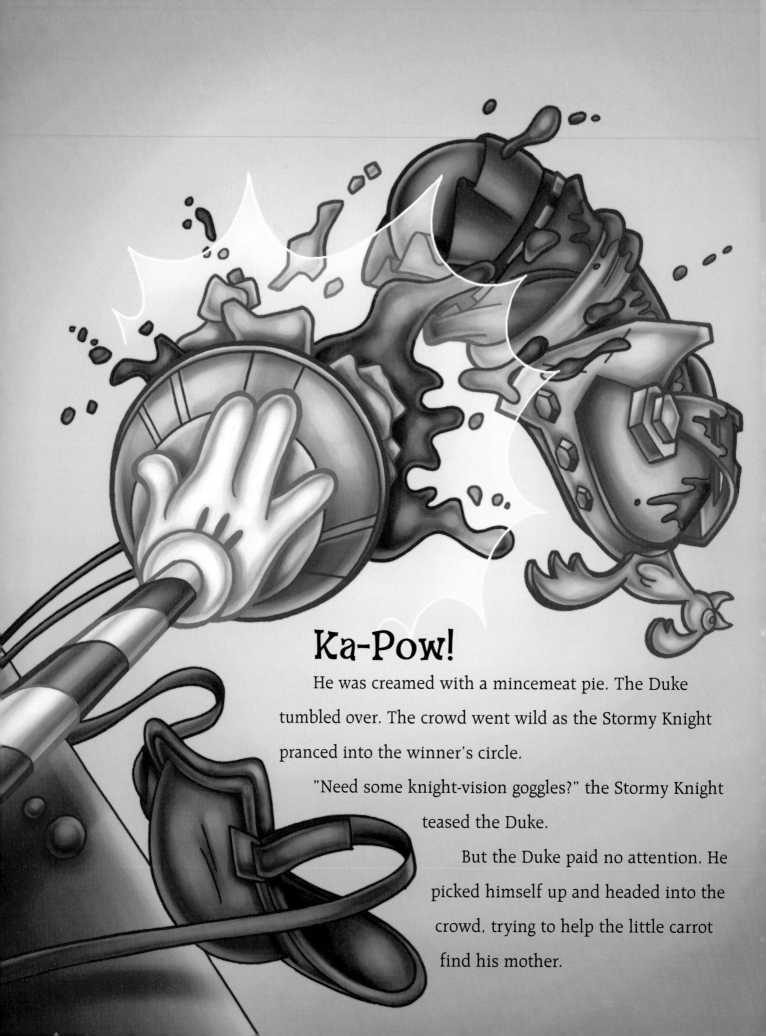

Ka-Pow!

He was creamed with a mincemeat pie. The Duke tumbled over. The crowd went wild as the Stormy Knight pranced into the winner's circle.

"Need some knight-vision goggles?" the Stormy Knight teased the Duke.

But the Duke paid no attention. He picked himself up and headed into the crowd, trying to help the little carrot find his mother.

By the end of the day, after a thousand pies had been hurled, it was time to name the champion. Traditionally, the queen tossed a bouquet of flowers to the fair maidens in the stadium. The maiden who caught the flowers was allowed to choose the champion from all the winners.

The queen hurled the bouquet of flowers high into the air, and they tumbled down, down, down...

The crowd gasped when they saw who caught the bouquet. But the queen stood and said, "My dear, you have the honor of choosing a champion from the winners."

Petunia stepped forward and stared at all the knights in the winner's circle. The Silent Knight, the Late Knight, the Stormy Knight, the Twelfth Knight, one of the Three Dog Knights, and the Hard Day's Knight waited impatiently.

"Pick me!" they called. "I deserve to get **FIRST!**"

After Petunia looked them over carefully, she took a deep breath.

"I have decided to name today's champion . . .

THE DUKE OF SCONE!"

She draped the golden, pie-shaped medal over the head of a very stunned cucumber.

All at once, people started shouting. "You can't give the medal to a loser!"

Petunia bravely stepped up to the microphone to address them. "The Duke should receive first place because he is the true champion. You see, today he was the only one who truly put **others** first. Whenever someone lost, the Duke was always there to help the loser up! That's more important than winning a contest. That's winning in God's eyes."

"You have chosen wisely," said the Queen. "How did you ever notice what the Duke was doing?"

"I am a Rhubarbarian," Petunia blushed. "I get teased and pushed away a lot. So when I see someone who puts others first, it's not difficult to remember."

The crowd stood up and cheered.

The Duke of Scone was a knight whom many would remember. Not because his name would go up in knight lights. Not because he was a starry knight. The Duke of Scone was a knight to remember because he was a **GOOD** knight, a legend in his land.

JOIN THE **TOURNAMENT OF PIES** BY USING YOUR EAGLE EYES. THERE ARE **5** DIFFERENCES BETWEEN THE TOP AND BOTTOM PICTURES. CAN YOU FIND THEM ALL?

THE ROYAL RHYME TIME CHALLENGE

The Kingdom needs your help! Can you find 3 pictures that rhyme with "Pie" and 3 pictures that rhyme with "Knight?"

Veggie Value to Share

GOD ASKS US TO PUT OTHERS' NEEDS AHEAD OF OUR OWN. DO YOU REMEMBER TIMES WHEN YOU PUT OTHERS FIRST?

ANSWERS: Pie: tie, fly, sky. Knight: white, light, kite.